MURDER AT THE MANOR

SHELLY WOTA

authorHOUSE®

Shelly Wota

AuthorHouse™
1663 Liberty Drive
Bloomington, IN 47403
www.authorhouse.com
Phone: 1 (800) 839-8640

This is a work of fiction. All of the characters, names, incidents, organizations, and dialogue in this novel are either the products of the author's imagination or are used fictitiously.

Published by AuthorHouse 08/22/2019

ISBN: 978-1-7283-2443-2 (sc)
ISBN: 978-1-7283-2442-5 (e)

Library of Congress Control Number: 2019912486

Print information available on the last page.

I would like to dedicate this book to my mom,
I would like to thank Chester, Libby and Angie
for all their help, much appreciated.

CHAPTER 1

The village of Cockernhoe, near Luton, is north of London about an hour drive. It is just a small village, with ten cottages and a small church, and is approximately a twenty-minute walk to the Beavington's estate, or a ten-minute bike ride. The estate is far away enough to give it a sense of being private but without being too far removed from the village residents, who over the years, had themselves or family members work there. Mr. Keyes, Sr. (a London solicitor) is driving up to meet with longtime clients, Philip & Mary Beavington. With him is his son, Jr. Keyes. "Why did you say we have to take this drive again, father?" asked Jr. in a bored voice. "I must get the Beavingtons to sign these papers before they leave for Europe," replied Sr. Keyes. He knows Jr. is not happy about having to take over his position, but his wife is very insistent that he retires soon, (he will be 76 years old). She wants to enjoy their later years in the South of France, where they spent their honeymoon. Sr. Keyes is counting the days. "But why me?" moaned Jr., "You have other junior staff, why not one of them?" Sr. repeats what he has done numerous times this past week, "You are my only heir, and it's a tradition that you take over from me. Also please remember, you will need to drive up at least once a week while the Beavingtons are away to keep an eye on things. You must admit, it is a beautiful drive," stated Sr. Keyes as he points out a small grove of trees surrounding a lake. "Who cares about scenery," mumbled Jr. The only good thing that would come out of this day is that he could renew his acquaintance with Alicia, the Beavington's soon to be an 18-year-old daughter. If he remembered correctly, Alicia was a nice looking girl with shoulder length blond hair and sparkling blue eyes. She would make any lord of the manor proud, and that is the plan Jr. has. He knows Mr. Beavington wants to settle a sum of money on her for her 18th birthday and also to arrange that the remainder would be hers upon his and his wife's death. Since Alicia is home now for a term break from the girl's school she is attending in London, Jr. decides it's the time to put his plan into action. Since the Beavingtons plan to throw Alicia a big birthday party, there will be a lot to prepare. As the Beavingtons only employ a small staff, they will have to hire residents from the nearby village to help. With such a small family and the Beavingtons not wanting to farm, they do not need to employ as much staff as their ancestors did, when there were several children and the estate had to sustain them.

They have a married couple, the housekeeper and butler, Mr. & Mrs. Locke, and their daughter, Gina, who is just a few months younger than Alicia. Gina's father, the butler, is not her biological father, Mr. Beavington, is. Gina also has beautiful blond hair but, with medium hazel eyes.

When Mrs. Beavington became pregnant with Alicia, she was ill a lot and because Mr. Beavington was so worried about her, he started drinking. One night in a drunken stupor, he came upon Mrs. Locke in the kitchen and forced himself upon her. After a few months, she had to tell Mr. Locke that she was expecting since Mr. Locke was incapable of fathering children. They confronted Mr. Beavington, who was so upset by his behavior he understood if they called the police. But both Locke's loved their home so that if it were made known Mrs. Beavington would be just devastated and of course it would put a blemish on the family name. They came to an agreement where Mr. Beavington would pay medical expenses and contribute to Gina's upbringing, as long as no one else found out. They were able to keep their secret for many years, but one day Gina found some papers and questioned her parents. They had no choice but to tell her since she would be turning 18 soon and Mr. Beavington had planned to settle some money on her also, so the Locke's would also be signing some papers that Sr. Keyes was bringing. The Beavingtons also employ a groundsman, Mr. Chestermere, a tall thin man who wears his moustache and beard in the same fashion he did during the Suez Crisis. He does not live at the manor but in the village. He is a bachelor who lives in the cottage his parents lived in and their parents before them. He has lived in Cockernhoe all his life except when attending school in London and for the short time that he lived abroad while in the services.

He goes out to the manor daily and if he ever needs any help with heavy lifting, he employs one or two of the village lads.

A month after her parents' departure, Alicia finished school, which meant she would be living on the estate full time. She was soon to be 18 years old and was much flattered by the attention of Jr. Keyes. He got into the habit of bringing her small gifts every time he came out to the estate. He's so romantic she tells herself. Her parents had told her that Jr. would be in charge while they were away. Jr. even took Alicia out for a short drive in his new car. But, he was also seen to pay attention to the housekeeper's daughter, Gina.

Little did Jr. know that Alicia and Arthur (the boy from the village who helps Mr. Chestermere on a part-time basis) had formed a friendship and were spending a lot of time together. Arthur had been persuading Alicia to tell her parents of their "love," but with the class distinction, Alicia knew her parents wouldn't approve of Arthur. She told him they would have to wait until she turned 21, then they can do whatever they want. When Jr. found out, he cruelly told Alicia that Arthur is her half-brother, so any notions of a romance were out of the question. To prove his point, he showed her Arthur's birth certificate.

CHAPTER 2

Mr. & Mrs. Beavington have recently returned from a 3-month European trip where they bought several antique items to add to their collection. They brought several of the smaller pieces home with them and are having the larger pieces shipped later. One such small piece was a cigar size box with Egyptian hieroglyphics on the sides and top, and it was locked. Another small box held a variety of keys. Jr. Keyes had come to the manor to catalog these items and take another opportunity to visit with Alicia. Jr. knew of what her parents will be settling upon her at her 18th birthday celebration, and since he was dissatisfied with his work, (catering to the whims of the wealthy), he has dreams of marrying Alicia and becoming lord of the manor.

The grounds on the Beavington estate are not as extensive as in the days of the former Beavingtons. These owners have let nature take over; they just need Mr. Chestermere to control the growth, keeping it well trimmed. Up until the curve in the lane, the grounds look wild and abandoned. But once past that curve, you can see where they are well kept. There are rows of flora along the drive leading to the house. The garden to the east side of the manor has been well organized with small shrubs along the sidewalk going towards the back of the house. The vegetable garden at the south of the house is smaller than it was at one time; it's just big enough to supply the current needs of the household, with some to donate to those in need.

Also on the south side of the home is a rather large greenhouse. This is where the Beavingtons have their exotic plants and flowers housed. Mr. Chestermere did wonder at why, but he will admit it is beautiful to see. Shortly after their return, the Beavington's were showing signs of fatigue, they were losing weight, and their skin took on a greenish tinge. They just accredited it to the very busy trip they recently returned from. Sr. Keyes and Mrs. Locke both noticed the change and suggested putting off the party, but the Beavingtons were adamant, as was Jr... Things finally seemed to be going his way.

Alicia had been consulting with him about what she could do with some or all the money her parents were giving her. Within two weeks the Beavingtons had succumbed to their ailment. They both died in their sleep. The party was postponed. Sr. Keyes proceeded with arrangements for burial, while Jr. took on the role to be Alicia's strength. Understandably, Alicia was distressed, her parents were away for three months, and she barely got to be with them before they pass away. Mrs. Locke had noticed that Alicia had not been eating well and knew she often cried herself to sleep. Mr. Locke and Mr. Chestermere had witnessed an argument between Alicia and Gina a few days later. Jr. had come by and persuaded Alicia to walk with him in the garden.

With his plans to become Lord of the Manor, Alicia would be in a vulnerable state, and he hoped she would agree to a private wedding ceremony. She was so upset that she pulled away from Jr. and ran away, crying.

Gina told her mother, who insisted that it is just stress for Alicia, and all will be well. After all, she had just lost both parents. While her parents had been away, Alicia was very demanding of the staff since she completed school. She wanted everything just perfect for when her parents would return. She especially demanded a lot of Gina who also had school to attend, but she was close enough that she could ride her bike then catch a trolley. Gina and Alicia's relationship had been like they were sisters until about age 15 when Alicia went away for her education to a boarding school in London. Understandably, their relationship would change since they are both from different worlds. (Alicia's aristocratic heritage and Gina coming from serving families.) Alicia became more of a snob, but the final breakdown of their friendship happened when Alicia's parents told her who Gina's birth father was and that he was paying for her education, among other things.

During the Beavington's absence, Jr. Keyes was taking over as family solicitor since his father Sr. Keyes was preparing to retire. He did not like what he had to do but getting to know Gina was a distraction. Gina's parents noticed the growing acquaintance and hoped marriage would come of it.

It was motivating for Jr. because he knew of Gina's future financial situation. Although Gina was a wonderful person, Jr. had higher aspirations; he wanted to be lord of the manor and that meant he needed to woo Alicia.

Mr. & Mrs. Locke were loyal to the Beavingtons but would prefer that their daughter marry Jr. Keyes, so they tried to put them together whenever Jr. came to the manor. Mr. Chestermere also noticed the amount of time Jr. spent with Gina and realized that nothing good could come of it and as well he noticed the attention Jr. was paying to Alicia, again knowing that nothing good could come of it. Arthur had been trying to get Alicia to inform her parents of their "love." She said that their "love" was forbidden. "Why do you say that," pleaded Arthur. They think I am too young to get married. Arthur angrily stated, "it may be because I am the hired help. They must think I'm after your money." "I have to wait until I'm 21. Alicia told Arthur, "then I can do what I want and marry whomever I want."

CHAPTER 3

A few nights after the Beavington's funerals, there was a severe storm with very strong winds. It was late September, the season when it would rain more than it would be clear. Mr. Chestermere was particularly worried about 2 of Mrs. Beavington's new acquisitions that he had transplanted in the corner near the greenhouse; where over the years during any heavy rainstorm the area could become flooded. He and his helper had repaired what was needed so they would be able to plant in that area. So he came to the manor early to check on them. He not only found them in place, and no worse for wear, but he also found Alicia. She was dead, still dressed in her previous day's clothes and clutching something in her hand.

Apparently, she had gone up to her room her usual time which was about 10 pm, and because of the strong winds, no one heard anything unusual. Gina said it had started raining about midnight because when she went down to the kitchen for a glass of milk and happened to glance out of the window at the wind and rain.

By the time Mr. Chestermere realized it, he had walked around the area, probably covering or messing up what could lead to finding out what had happened. He ran around to the back of the house and started pounding on the kitchen door. "Open up, open up" he frantically yelled.

Since it was still early, Mr. Locke came to the door with a cleaver in his hand, cursing, "there better be a good reason, waking people up so early," he shouted as he yanked the door open. Mr. Chestermere almost had a heart attack, seeing Mr. Locke still dressed in his nightclothes brandishing a cleaver. He also noticed Mrs. Locke peaking from around the kitchen door clutching a rolling pin. "Call emergency," he screamed, "she's dead." Poor Mrs. Locke thought he meant Gina, and she almost fainted, but then realized that Gina was standing behind her. "Who is dead?" yelled Mr. Locke? Mr. Chestermere was babbling something about she's green; she's green. "It's Miss Alicia, call emergency. While Mr. Locke was calling emergency, Mrs. Locke put on a pot of tea. She felt she needed to keep busy until the police came. Her hands were so shaky. Mr. Locke also called the Keyes, but only Sr. Keyes was home. Jr. walked in a few minutes later, looking the worse for wear. It looked like he had got caught in the rain and had slept in his clothes. When Gina offered him a cup of tea, he gave her a pleading look as he reached out to touch her hand. Mr. Chestermere noticed the movement and realized that maybe a few things he had been witnessing over the past few months meant something. No one thought to ask how he could have driven there so fast since they knew he lived in London. Even Gina seemed nervous. Everyone knew about the argument she had with Alicia the night before.

It had something to do with Mr. Beavington arranging to pay for her schooling and daily upkeep. Alicia could never pass up an opportunity to remind Gina she was just one of the working class. The police and ambulance arrived about 20 minutes later. They had to drive from the village of Rumforton since Cockernhoe does not house either. Mr. Chestermere rushed out to direct them to the area where he had found the body. He had covered Alicia's body with his coat. When Detective Constable Kate Rainey and Detective Sergeant Bill Dunes came into the kitchen, all the staff were looking frightened. DC Rainey quickly reassured them and accepted a cup of tea from Mrs. Locke. DS Dunes was out with the paramedics to take pictures of the scene. They would have to await the arrival of the ME, who would be coming from London.

DS Dunes returned to the kitchen with Mr. Chestermere, and Mrs. Locke offered them both a cup of tea. During all this, Jr. was sitting at the table with his head in his hands. He looked more worried than scared. He insisted on calling his father since he felt out of his depth. Mr. Locke assured Jr. that Sr. Keyes was on his way. He had never had anything to do with death before and especially since he knew the deceased so well, he wasn't sure what to do next. Could he be mourning his lost opportunity of becoming lord of the manor? He stood up and gruffly demanded, "How long is this going to take?"

DC Rainey apologized for the wait and said that DS Dunes would take his statement next. At that moment Sr. Keyes arrived. Jr. looked relieved. Sr. Keyes and DC Rainey conferred a moment then Sr. Keyes went out to meet with DS Dunes.

CHAPTER 4

D r. Mike Burns, ME, arrived and set about doing a brief exam of the body and crime scene. Because of the harsh rains, there likely wouldn't be any signs of blood. Dr. Burns decided to check for any other wounds, like a knife or gunshot. Alicia's hair stuck to her face because of the way she was laying in the fresh damp earth that Mr. Chestermere used to transplant the rose bushes. Dr. Burns also noticed the green tinge on Alicia's face. It was the same as that on Alicia's parents. He had his crew prepare her body to be brought to the lab for the autopsy.

Meanwhile, DS Dunes was looking around the greenhouse, which was just about 15 feet away from where Alicia was laying. The rain would have washed away any sign of footprints, but he noticed the door to the greenhouse was slightly ajar. Had the gardener left it open or did the wind do it, or was that where Alicia was hurt and was trying to get to the house for help? He needed to call in more officers to go over the entire greenhouse. He would also need someone who knew about plants and whatever else was stored in a greenhouse. He decided to call his finance, Professor Liz Bloom, who teaches at U of Essex. Dr. Burns, with a helper, finished the preliminary exam and was leaving. DS Dunes then noticed a young man exiting the greenhouse carrying a jacket and shouted: "what are you doing in there?"

The young man was so startled that he started stammering about leaving his jacket last night and just came by to get it. Clearly, he did not know about Alicia, but when DS Dunes told him, he almost fainted. It seems that this lad had more than just friendly feelings for Alicia. DS Dunes brought him into the kitchen for a cup of tea.

DC Rainey wished to talk to Mrs. Locke and Gina separately, so she brought Gina to the library with Sr. Keyes present, since she was not yet 18. She was not just nervous; she was downright scared. Having Sr. Keyes in the room with her helped calm her, but poor Mrs. Locke needed her smelling salts and had to sit down while waiting for her turn to be questioned.

Jr., the lad from the village and Mr. Chestermere had been permitted to go home but to be available for further questioning the next day. Jr. was so shaky he needed to calm down before attempting the drive home.

DS Dunes left a police officer to stay with the family during the night. He advised everyone not to talk to each other about their questioning. Mrs. Locke felt they need to be busy, so she made up a cold dinner, although no one was hungry enough to eat. It had been an exhausting day.

Mr. Locke mentioned to DS Dunes that he overheard an argument Alicia had with Gina a few days after her parents passed away. He attributed it to stress and mourning, so he did not ask Gina about it.

During the preliminary investigation of the greenhouse, the police made a list of all opened containers to verify which ones might hold poisonous chemicals. They will send the list to Professor Liz Bloom of the U of Essex.

CHAPTER 5

DS Dunes was asking Mr. Chestermere who that young man was that he brought into the kitchen. "His name is Arthur, Arthur Graves, one of the lads I hire to help with heavy work," replied Mr. Chestermere. "He is a hard worker, gets along with everyone, given his background." "Did he get along with Mr. & Mrs. Beavington?" questioned DS Dunes. "Did he have much contact with Miss Alicia?" DS Dunes made himself a note to look into Arthur's past. "When was he last here?" he asked. "Also, if you could give me the names of any other person who had access to the grounds, especially the greenhouse, that would be much appreciated."

Mr. Chestermere felt he should mention that he believed that Miss Alicia and Arthur were too friendly with each other. "Why do you think that?" queried DS Dunes. "Well," begins Mr. Chestermere, "while Mr. & Mrs. Beavington was away and when Miss Alicia was home from school, I would see her and Arthur talking behind the greenhouse quite often. I would make excuses to separate them since I didn't think it would be proper if they became more than just friends. "Why do you think that?" asked DS Dunes. "It's the class distinction thing," replied Mr. Chestermere. "I know it's the 1980's, but the Beavingtons were ruled by it."

Arthur's stepfather, Malcolm, lives in a cottage in the village, like

I do," pointed out Mr. Chestermere. "He married Arthur's mother when Arthur was just a baby."

"His father and grandfather both worked at the manor in their day. I don't know if the stories I heard are true, but they were both fired. I've never heard why, but the Beavingtons would not hire a Trowbridge after that. You can ask any of the older folk in the village. I can hire Arthur because his last name is the same as his stepfathers, which is Graves." "What about his mother?" queried DS Dunes?

"I haven't seen her in a while, the villagers said she went to London to stay with her sick mother, but the last I heard, her mother had convalesced." "Who gave you this information?" asked DS Dunes. "Her neighbor Lois; who is also her best friend," added Mr. Chestermere. "Lois also wondered why her friend hasn't returned since the news about her mom is good. But knowing whom she will come back to, it's understandable. Lois has even tried phoning Maggie, but was always told that she is out and will get the message." "Please explain what you mean by it's understandable," asked DS Dunes. "It's her husband, Malcolm; he's a lazy, cruel man, who is jealous of the high regard Maggie is held by the villagers. He insists that Arthur has to give over most of his wages for the household," stated Mr. Chestermere.

"Can I ask if you have any idea who may have done such a cruel thing to Alicia?" Mr. Chestermere quietly asked. "Sorry, can't say," replied DS Dunes, "ongoing investigation and all." "If you think of anything else, please give me a call," stated DS Dunes, as he hands Mr. Chestermere his card.

DS Dunes asked Sr. Keyes, who was in control of the Beavington's estate. "My son Jr. is," replied Sr. Keyes. "Since I'll be retiring soon Jr. has been out here with me many times. He will be taking over from me; he knows what's involved." "I heard that he and Alicia have become quite close," stated DS Dunes. "Is there more to their relationship than that of solicitor and client?" "He's never said anything either to his mother or me, but anything is possible," replied Sr. Keyes. "I also heard Jr. and Gina have gotten closer," pointed out DS Dunes. "What do you think?" "No, knowing Jr., he would not become too attached to Gina." insisted Sr. Keyes. "Why is that?" questioned DS Dunes." Jr. is a great guy, but he can be snobby, the class distinction thing, you know," admitted his father.

After DC Rainey interviewed the Locke's, she got the impression that Mrs. Locke thought Jr. was only after Alicia's money. Mr. Locke did mention that Jr. came out to the estate several times a week. DC Rainey felt that the Locke's had hoped Jr. and Gina would make a match. Jr. would spend time with Gina, but that was only while Alicia was otherwise occupied. Those were the times Arthur was on the estate. DC Rainey returned to the manor the next morning. He told the Locke's he and his team needed to investigate further. He sent one team to Alicia's room, and another to check the Locke's rooms. DC Rainey would need to take more statements. Sr. & Jr. Keyes had been asked to return to explain the procedures to everyone.

The team found Alicia's diary hidden under a shoebox in her closet. DS Dunes had a quick look at the few of the entries days before her death. He would peruse it further at the mobile unit they had set up in Rumforton. He also had in his possession a locked cigar size box with Egyptian hieroglyphics. Maybe the key found in Alicia's clutched hand would fit the lock. The team searching Mr. Beavington's library found his will and the papers Sr. Keyes had brought for him to sign, settling other monies to Gina. Mr. Beavington did sign them, but Sr. Keyes had not legally authorized them; therefore, Gina would not be receiving any monies outside of what was stated in the will. That leaves Jr. Keyes as executor to Gina's money and the whole estate, since Alicia was an only child and no other family of the Beavington's could be found (if there were any) (a further search of the Beavington's papers may show something). There was a half-brother but no one had seen or heard of him in many years. When Mr. Beavington was just 16 years old, he had an alliance with the housemaid, Maggie (who is Arthur's mother). When it was noticed that she was pregnant she was fired and only a few people know what happened to her and the baby.

CHAPTER 6

D S Dunes went to the village to take Mr. Chestermere's statement. He felt it would be private and more relaxing. Experience showed him that some people could remember more outside the confines of the police station. Mr. Chestermere brought in a pot of tea and some biscuits. He sat in his favorite chair while DS Dunes seated himself on the sofa. All right, Mr. Chestermere, let's begin. What is your first name, for the record you understand? It's Henry, responded Mr. Chestermere. Okay, Henry, do you know if Jr. and Alicia were more than just friends?" he asked. "Or maybe Jr. and Gina? What can you tell me about them?" Remember, something you may consider unimportant may be very important. Anything would be of help in finding Alicia's murderer."

"It was the day after Mr. & Mrs. Beavington's funerals; I went to check up on a plant that had not been growing well. I had been trying some plant food I heard about from the gardener of the estate on the other side of my village. Mrs. Locke told me Alicia had been crying until quite late and that she hadn't answered her door when she brought up her breakfast tray. Mr. Locke said to just let her alone; she will eat when she's ready. As I was walking toward the area of the garden where the sick plant was, I heard voices. I realized they were Miss Alicia's and Miss Gina's." answered, Mr. Chestermere.

Alicia was very angry with Gina. It seemed like they both were seeking solitude in what had been Mr. & Mrs. Beavington's favorite area. Gina tried to comfort Alicia, but she would not allow it. She screamed at Gina; I hate you; I wish I never knew you. Miss Gina ran off crying. I had just had time to step behind the rugosa rose bush so she wouldn't see me. I was about to leave Alicia to her mourning when Jr. approached. I couldn't hear everything that was said, but I did hear Alicia scream, "What do you know about love? You probably want my money also.

Leave me alone; I love Arthur." Jr. tried to suggest that she forget Arthur, but Alicia wouldn't listen, so he handed her a piece of paper. "I hoped it wouldn't come to this, but you will see what I mean once you read it, it will prove Arthur is not the man for you." Alicia took a step back and sat down. She yelled at Jr." You're lying, how can you be so hateful?" She ran off crying. I waited for Jr. to leave, then I left, and when I went over to the small garden opposite the greenhouse, I came upon Alicia and Arthur. It was the area that they had met several times. Alicia thrust the piece of paper at him and asked, "Is it true? Are you my half-brother?" Arthur sounded quite angry when he asked her where she got that paper. "Jr. gave it to me. I think he's jealous and wants to break us up. She looked up at him with sad eyes and asked again, is it true? Did you know? Jr. said you are after my money, are you? If not, how would you support us? " cried Alicia. " I love you," said Arthur as he attempted to hug her.

But Alicia pulled away and screamed, "Leave me alone; I hate you all." I saw her run into the house. Mrs. Locke told me Alicia spent the afternoon in her room and asked that her supper be brought up on a tray. I stayed and had supper with the Lockes and left at about 9 pm. It had just started to rain." stated Mr. Chestermere. "Did you see Jr. or Arthur before you left?" inquired DS Dunes. "No, but I had assumed they both left after their confrontations with Alicia. What happens now?" Mr. Chestermere asked.

CHAPTER 7

"We will go over all the statements and evidence, confirm alibis and hope there was one tiny detail we missed. The longer it takes will minimize our success for an arrest," stated DS Dunes. "What happens to the estate? Can we carry on as usual?" Mr. Chestermere asked with a sad look on his face. "Sr. Keyes will oversee the day-to-day finances, as before. You must all try to continue your daily routine. Now that the coroner has released the body for burial; Sr. Keyes will be in touch about the funeral arrangements." answered DS Dunes.

DS Dunes and DC Rainey spend the next day at the mobile unit in Rumforton reviewing all statements and evidence. "Did an officer get the jacket from Arthur?" DS Dunes enquired of DC Rainey. "It's in the evidence box, Sir," replied DC Rainey. DS Dunes puts on gloves and removes the key that was found clutched in Alicia's hand, from an evidence bag along with the small box and her diary. He tried the key in the lock of the box, and it opened. Inside was just one folded piece of paper. Could it be the one Mr. Chestermere saw Jr. give Alicia, he wonders to himself? After reading the paper he exclaims, well! Well! "What is it?" questioned DC Rainey. "It's a birth certificate for Arthur, stating Mr. Beavington as the father. Poor Alicia, after all, she's suffered from the loss of both parents, to find out that the man she loves is her half-brother. It looks like there will be two inheritors to the Beavington estate.

First, we will have this certificate and Gina's certificate authenticated. By the way, did you notice anything unusual about Arthur's jacket?" questioned DS Dunes. "It's a size large and Arthur is definitely not a size large, so whose jacket is it and why was Arthur retrieving it?" questioned DC Rainey. "Have it, and the birth certificates send to our London lab for testing for DNA," responded DS Dunes. "Sure thing, Sir, shall I have some tea brought?" asked DC Rainey. "That would be great, thanks, with some biscuits," added DS Dunes.

DS Dunes settled in and said, "So, let's go through every statement bit by bit, starting with Sr. Keyes. His alibi checks out. Mr. & Mrs. Locke – they alibi each other and apart from hoping Gina would make a match with Jr. Keyes, I see no motive on their part. Since Mr. Beavington had already made arrangements for Gina, money could not be her motive, unless it's more personal. Maybe Gina had a crush on Arthur or vice versa, and Alicia did not like it. We will keep her in our sights. Now, there's Mr. Chestermere – what do you think? He said he heard the last conversation Alicia had. Could he be exaggerating? I don't know much about him, but since he left the service, he has led a very quiet life and never been married, with no troubles at work. Took some night courses, I assume for socializing. Then a couple of years ago he returned to the village. His father's parents left him their cottage. Shortly later, he got hired at the manor.

I guess those night courses must have had something to do with plants and things. I don't believe the Beavingtons would hire someone without knowledge of how to care for exotic plants. "Sir, do you think it's happenstance that Mr. Chestermere always seemed to be nearby to overhear any conversation Alicia has had with others?: asked DC Rainey. "Then we have Arthur – he had access to the estate, being Mr. Chestermere's helper. His family history with the Beavingtons makes me wonder. We'll need to dig deeper and question his mother, stepfather and more of the village people. We may even need to speak to his grandmother in London."

CHAPTER 8

When DS Dunes and his officer were in Cockernhoe to question villagers, they heard that Arthur's mother and stepfather, Malcolm, had left in a hurry the morning of the murder. Maggie's best friend thinks Maggie's mother may have taken ill again. She asked her to keep an eye on their cottage while they were away. DS Dunes asked how much luggage they took. "Enough for at least a week or so," replied Lois. "Do you have a key to their cottage?" questioned DS Dunes. "Do you think they killed Miss Alicia?" whispered Lois. "We have a warrant to search. It does seem a coincidence that they left in such a hurry, and I'll also need Maggie's mother's phone number and address," stated DS Dunes. "The sooner we can question them, the sooner we may be able to rule them out as suspects." "DS Dunes turns to Lois and asks if Arthur went with them?" "No," exclaimed Lois, "he was told not to leave by your officer." "Officer Olson will search for Arthur's parents' cottage while I go with Mr. Chestermere to question other villagers. But first I need to make a call to London to have them send someone to Arthur's grandmother's residence. Can I use your phone, Mr. Chestermere?" While DS Dunes was in Cockernhoe, the station in Rumforton received a call from London with the autopsy results. An officer from Rumforton drove to Cockernhoe to inform DS Dunes that he is supposed to call the London lab.

"How's it going, DS Dunes, bellowed Dr. Burns. We have a bit of a bad connection, so I'll get to the point. Alicia Beavington was not murdered; her death was considered an accident. Do you remember I told you I saw a greenish tinge on her parents, well, so did Alicia? They all died from contact with a highly fatal pesticide. Knowing that they worked so many hours in their greenhouse caring for their new acquisitions from abroad, they wanted to make sure they were healthy enough for transplanting." "So, why hasn't Mr. Chestermere been affected?" demanded DS Dunes. "He would know to use protective gear; obviously the Beavingtons did not.

Professor Liz Bloom can explain better. But with Alicia, she must have been trying to finish whatever her parents were working on. It would be a sort of grieving process for her to be so close to what was so important to her parents. None of the staff would have paid too much attention to the many hours she spent in the greenhouse; they would just want to leave her to her private mourning. She must have been feeling quite ill and tried to get to the house for help, but with the heavy rain and wind, it sapped the rest of her energy. Her death is officially considered accidental." "Thank you, Dr. Burns, could you have everything sent to the Rumforton station as soon as possible. I want to close this case."

DS Dunes turned to Officer Olson and said, "We're done here; it was not murder." "But sir, Officer Olson asks hesitantly, what about the key, that piece of paper about Arthur being a Beavington, and the conversations Mr. Chestermere overheard and that too large jacket, are you still going to interview the villagers to get information about Arthur's family, or do we just ignore all that?" "Well, we have to face the facts; Dr. Burns said her death was accidental. There is nothing more we can do unless a family member wants a further investigation and that could either be Gina or Arthur and I'm sure neither of them would want that to delay their receiving their inheritance. If the courts are satisfied, then I have to be," replied DS Dunes as he walks off with a shrug. As soon as I receive the official report, I'll go to the manor and explain to everyone. Thank you, Officer Olson, for all your help.

"There you are DS Dunes," pants Mr. Chestermere, as he hurries toward him. "Is everything all right?" "Since it's getting on, we'll quit for the day," replied DS Dunes. "Thanks for all your help. I'll be in touch."

Two days later everyone was sitting in the parlor. They had been requested to be there at 10 a.m. No one knows why, but only has to wait a few minutes before DS Dunes and DC Rainey enter. "Thank you all for coming, this won't take long," stated DS Dunes. "We can close this case. With the ME's report, it is officially considered an accidental death."

The men express their surprise with a sad look while Mrs. Locke and Gina start to cry. "What happened," begged Mrs. Locke. "The information I'm about to tell you is for your ears only, the public will hear that it was accidental," replied DS Dunes. "Alicia and her parents had been in contact with a potentially lethal pesticide and had not worn proper protective gear. It doesn't take much time before it seeps into their bodies, and the symptoms are so minor that a person would only think they were working too hard, so unless they go to a doctor, they had no chance of surviving. We're sorry for your loss. Sr. Keyes will explain what will happen next." As he and DS Rainey turn to leave, DS Dunes stops and turns back as if he had something else to say. "What is it, sir?' questioned DS Rainey. "I'm not sure," whispered DS Dunes, "but I feel I've forgotten something."

CHAPTER 9

Sr. Keyes explained that he would come back in a couple of days to read the will. Since Alicia had not made a will, they will adhere to what is stated in Mr. & Mrs. Beavington's wills. Jr. was silently cursing his misfortune of not becoming Lord of the Manor since poor Alicia is now gone, but he suddenly remembers one aspect of Mr. Beavington's bequeathments. He will need another look at that will before he acts because he thinks that Gina may come into more than at first decided, so he tells his father that he realized he has an appointment in London and must leave. Since Sr. Keyes has other business to see to before he would leave, it will give Jr. the time he needs to get to London. Once he reads the will again his dream of becoming Lord of the Manor still seemed attainable. Besides, he has always liked Gina and he knows she likes him, so he decided he would go back to the manor and speak to Gina.

After Sr. Keyes left, Gina went out to the garden and there Arthur found her. They both have gotten to know each other a bit over the past few months; even though Alicia had demanded most of his time when he wasn't helping Mr. Chestermere. Arthur believed he was the only other heir after what Alicia told him, so once Sr. Keyes reads the will it would only be a matter of time before he and Gina can set up housekeeping as Lord and Lady of the Manor. He has plans to make changes, especially concerning Mr. Chestermere.

Arthur then would be able to order him around until he finds a replacement, definitely someone younger. Only a few more days, he reminds himself. He goes in search of Gina, and much to his dismay he sees her and Jr. talking. It looks cozy. He begins to feel angry, first Alicia now Gina. Jr. probably just wants Gina's inheritance. Dam the fool. Doesn't he realize that with Gina being only the help's daughter, she probably would not inherit much? But, Jr. could know something or else why would he be here. He wanders off thinking of what he can do.

Meanwhile, Jr.'s attentions to Gina are refused. She said she has feelings for someone else. "Who is it?" begged Jr.? "Is he from a good family, or is he after your inheritance? Please tell me." "It's Arthur," whispered Gina. "He loves me, I just know it." "Did he tell you that before Alicia passed away, or after?" questioned Jr. "Because I know for a fact that Arthur told Alicia that he loved her. It looks like he "loves" whoever has money. Please think about it, talk to your parents or my father; but don't rush into anything. What with all that has been happening, you need to step back and give yourself time to mourn.

If Arthur truly loves you, he would understand." Gina nods and whispered, "you're probably right, thanks, Jr." Wow, Jr. says to himself after Gina leaves. She obviously doesn't know that Arthur is her half-brother, therefore the co-inheritor. I need to think of something.

They cannot be allowed to be alone. It's only 48 hours until the reading of the will, then, we'll see. Satisfied with this idea, Jr. smiles and returns to the manor for tea.

Meanwhile, Arthur is wandering around the manor grounds as if it was already the lord. He has so many ideas floating around in his head that he doesn't notice Jr. approaching him. "What are you playing at?" demanded Jr. "First Alicia, now Gina. Does Gina even know you are her half-brother?" Seeing the angry look on your face, I suspected not." snapped Jr. "You know she will find out tomorrow. She is the co-inheritor to the Beavington estate. She thinks you love her. She needs to know the truth, you better tell her tonight or I will," demanded Jr.

Arthur stomped off, cursing his bad luck. First Alicia; now Gina. It's that interfering Jr.

Since Gina is my half-sister, I will probably split the estate, but that won't work, I want it all. I deserve it, mumbled Arthur. Maybe she'll agree to be my partner in the running of the estate, not an equal partner, of course. I'll need to talk to her as soon as I can. Even though we can't get married, I can play up on her feelings for me. I will need her to trust me completely so her parents won't object. We would make a good brother/sister team, and then when I get married I will buy her out.

After all, she may want to marry one day and have a family. Her parents may be an obstacle, but I will cross that bridge when I come to it. My main objective is Gina, and then her parents will follow. I may try to convince Gina that her parents should go on a long holiday. So much depends on tomorrow.

CHAPTER 10

Arthur didn't get a chance to talk to Gina. She had stayed close to her parents all evening. I need to talk to her, mumbled Arthur. As he starts walking home, he notices that Gina's light was on, so he got a ladder and put it up under her window. Meanwhile, Mr. Chestermere is bidding Mr. & Mrs. Locke goodnight. Since he and Arthur live in the same village and knowing that Arthur left just a few minutes before him, Mr. Chestermere thought he would overtake him. By the time he arrived at the village outskirts he still hadn't seen Arthur. During that time Arthur had climbed the ladder and was knocking on Gina's window. "What are you doing," whispered Gina. "If my parents saw you, you would be in great trouble, go away." "But I need to talk to you," begged Arthur. "Tomorrow," insists Gina, "after Mr. Keyes leaves." "It can't wait, please come down to the greenhouse, it will only take a few minutes." "Okay," mumbled Gina, "I'll be down in 5 minutes, be sure to put the ladder away." She arrived to find Arthur pacing. "What took you so long?" growled Arthur. "Dad was still up, so I had to go around. What is so important that it couldn't wait?" growled Gina. She felt bad, but she couldn't wait until the reading of the will; she was wondering how much she would inherit. "Gina, you know I care for you like a sister, so what I have to say will come as a shock to you, but you have to believe me." "Why are you changing your mind?

So what Jr. said must be true, you're only after my money. I have been such a fool. I hate you," she screamed, "leave me alone." "Gina, please, it wouldn't be right for us to be together," begged Arthur. "Why?" cried Gina. "I'm so sorry that I have to be the one to tell you, I assumed your parents would have. You and I have the same father; we are half-brother and sister. I didn't know until Jr. told me yesterday. Please believe me." he begged. "I don't believe you," screamed Gina. " What proof do you have?" "I have none, but ask Jr.," answered Arthur, he just told me, or maybe you should ask your parents." "But I do not believe him, maybe he just doesn't want us to be together, or knowing what you might inherit, he wants you."

"After all, his father's office will be handling the reading of the will, I'm sure he has read it," added Arthur. Gina nods, remembering the conversation she had with Jr. the day before. "I don't see how he thinks he will profit by this," added Gina.

"This is too much to think about; I'm going in. Goodnight, Arthur." "Wait, begged Arthur," what are you going to do? "I'll talk to my parents first thing in the morning," replied Gina," goodnight." Arthur walked away as if in a daze. He has so much on his mind that he forgot he rode his bike.

After a sleepless night, Gina confronted her parents first thing. Sr. Keyes won't be arriving until 10 am so she has time to find out why. "Gina, are you ill? exclaimed her mother as she attempted to check for a fever.

"Don't," muttered Gina, as she takes a step back." I didn't sleep very well last night. She looks at her parents and in a teary voice asked, is Arthur my half-brother? Noticing the look on their faces, she cried, "Why didn't you tell me?" We care very much for each other and one day wanted to get married. Now all this; it's sick, I have fallen in love with my half-brother, I feel so dirty. Mom, dad, my heart is broken." sobbed Gina. "He will probably inherit this house and ask us to leave, what are we going to do? "Remember, Gina, you are also Mr. Beavington's child, you may inherit half, stated her mother. "Why wouldn't it be split equally?" "Do you think so, mom? Asked Gina, "but I don't think I could live here with him knowing how I felt. I would feel awkward."

"Maybe he could buy my half then we could move away," suggested Gina. "Don't worry yourself over what may not be," said Mr. Locke. "We'll just wait until the reading of the will, and go on from there." If we have to move, so be it." We will have to wait and see."

CHAPTER 11

Everyone was nervously waiting for Sr. Keyes to arrive. Arthur kept making side glances at Gina, who had moved her chair away from where her parents sat. Jr. had a smug look on his face. Only Mr. Chestermere seemed calm.

"Good morning everyone," called Sr. Keyes as he enters the library. "You know why we are here, so I'll just get started. You can ask questions later. This is an unusual situation where all members of an immediate family are deceased. Normally a husband would leave his estate to his wife and any offspring, but since they are also deceased, his estate would go to the next surviving family member. I can see the confused looks on all your faces so I will tell you that we did find a family member who will inherit the entire estate except for any separate annuities bequeathed to others. As you may not know, the late Mrs. Beavington (nee Mary Smythe) was born in this area, but when her father passed away, and while she was still a child, her mother moved them to London to be with family where she later remarried to Mr. Chestermere and they had a son. Since Mary's mother and step-father were of the same social circle as Mr. Beavington's family, they had to meet. Mr. Beavington was attending Oxford and would meet Mary occasionally at social events. They got to know each other and eventually married.

I know, I know, what does that have to do with it, you're asking yourselves. I'll get to it. The son I mentioned earlier is the late Mrs. Beavington's half-brother. We'll get to that. But first I will mention the bequeaths from Mrs. Beavington. To Mr. & Mrs. Locke, £10,000, to their daughter, Gina, £4,000, and to Arthur, who has been a great help to Mr. Chestermere, £1500. All her personal items, such as jewelry, clothes, etc. will go to the half-brother to do with as he chooses.

Mr. Beavington made a few separate bequeaths: to Mr. & Mrs. Locke, for all their care and love: £10,000.00, for Gina and Arthur, he will pay for any further education they wish to pursue, up until they turn 25 years old. Now for the individual who will inherit the remainder of the Beavington estate; our Mr. Henry Chestermere." Amid all the surprising comments, DS Dunes entered. "Why is he here?" demanded Jr. "It is because of DS Dunes investigations that we confirmed that Mr. Chestermere is Mrs. Beavington's half-brother," stated Sr. Keyes. "Are there any questions?" "Do we have to move out, and when?" inquired Mr. Locke. "From this point on, Mr. Chestermere is the owner of the Beavington Estate. He will be meeting with each of you in the next few days. Until then, everything will continue as before." remarked Sr. Keyes. "I want to thank everyone for attending. Mr. Chestermere and Jr., would you please remain behind, I have some papers for you to sign."

As everyone was leaving DS Dunes had the opportunity to observe their expressions. Mr. Chestermere was hard to read, DS Dunes imagined that he would be surprised not looking calm. Mr. & Mrs. Locke certainly looked surprised and hopeful as did Gina. Arthur looked confused and slightly put out, whereas Jr. looked to be deep in thought. He realized that since Gina did not inherit any part of the estate that he would wish her well and he knew that his dream of becoming lord of the manor, would not come to fruition, so he would have to reevaluate his dreams for his future. He was certain that Mr. Chestermere would keep him as the solicitor for Beavington Manor since his father was retiring. DS Dunes thought that Mr. Chestermere should look surprised, not calm. It was as if he knew that he would be inheriting Beavington Manor. DS Dunes had the feeling that he would be returning to the manor at some time soon.

Arthur decided to wait until his conversation with Mr.

Chestermere before he made any plans. As much as the work with Mr. Chestermere was difficult at times, Arthur realized he actually liked working with his hands; maybe he would continue his education with the money he inherited and either come back to work for Mr. Chestermere or hire on somewhere else. It will all depend on Mr. Chestermere's plans.

CHAPTER 12.

After everyone else left, Sr. Keyes suggested to Mr. Chestermere that he take up residence at the manor as soon as possible. He will need to accustom himself to being in charge and the estate books are there. Sr. Keyes assured him that he is free to make any changes, not just to the running of the household, but anything to do with the land. After all, he assured Mr. Chestermere that all of this is yours. Maybe he would like to look into another type of farming. He also asked that he consider keeping Jr. on as solicitor but would understand if he wanted a different firm to attend to all his legal matters. Sr. Keyes informed Mr. Chestermere that this would be his last official duty once all papers are signed. As he and Jr. were leaving, he wished Lord Chestermere luck. Jr. winced slightly at that comment.

Lord Chestermere left word that he would return for dinner. He felt he needed time to be alone to gather his thoughts and collect his few belongings that are worth bringing to his new home. All was quiet. The Lockes in the kitchen, each with a cup of tea, Gina was in her room, and Arthur had already left for the village. When Lord Chestermere looked back (at his new home), the sun was high in the sky and birds were chirping. This is mine, he said in a half whisper, all mine. Finally, he said to himself as he set off to the village. Meanwhile, Jr. was in deep thought as he was walking home.

DS Dunes felt that Lord Chestermere was too calm after hearing he was now the sole owner of the estate. He made a mental note to dig deeper into Mr. Chestermere's past up until he started working for the Beavingtons.

Over the next few days, Lord Chestermere acquainted himself with the manor's books. He had an idea about the land but will need to wait until after the interviews he plans on having with the others. He intends to ask the Lockes to stay on and ask Gina what further education she would like to pursue. Also, if Arthur plans further schooling, Lord Chestermere would need to hire another helper. It's going to be a busy week.

In London, DS Dunes had checked several universities to find out which one Henry Chestermere had attended. After what seemed like making endless calls, DS Dunes finally located it. It was the University of Oxford. They compiled a list of teachers who were there at that time and one of fellow students. DS Dunes and DC Rainey decided to interview the teachers first. The list was small since too many years have passed and many were deceased. They were told that Henry Chestermere was a quiet student who got above average marks. He got along with fellow students but had only a few close friends. They also confirmed what the teachers had said. Of those students, one died during the Suez Crisis (he was fighting alongside Henry). Overall, it looks like Henry Chestermere was without blemish. DS Dunes has names of two ex-girlfriends who had dated Henry for longer periods.

DS Dunes did see another side of Henry but nothing that raised a red flag. If Henry had anything to hide, no one knew what it was. After having spent time with him, DS Dunes concluded that it is entirely possible that Mr. Chestermere was hiding something. Their next inquiries would be the years Henry was in the service.

DS Dunes decided that they would have to work backward to locate names and address of any friends or acquaintances. It would take time, but since DS Dunes had the feeling that something wasn't quite right, he felt obligated to find the truth. He did get a name and address of a lady who was the college registrar when Henry would have been registered. She was 98 years old and living in a senior's Extendicare facility. He does not feel she would be of much help, but any help would be welcome at this point. DS Dunes brought an older female constable with him, hoping that Miss James would feel more comfortable talking with a female. They were made welcome at the facility, and DS Dunes was surprised at how alert Miss James was. But, he did not allow himself to be too hopeful. After tea and biscuits had been brought in, DS Dunes sat to the side to let Constable Stephanie Martin take the lead. He did not want it to feel like an interrogation, but more like a friendly visit. After several cups of tea and what seemed like a ton of biscuits, DS Dunes and Constable Martin left the residence with a few names. Miss James was a fount of information. DS Dunes was very grateful.

He and Constable Martin went back to the office to plan the next stage of the investigation. One name was that of a nurse who had just started her job at the University of Oxford about the time Henry started attending.

CHAPTER 13

The nurse had nothing relevant to add. Henry only visited her a few times, and they were for the usual rugby injuries. The more he thought about it; the more DS Dunes felt that something was not right concerning Henry Chestermere.

From the counselor who worked at the University of Oxford, DS Dunes found out that Mr. Chestermere suffered from a form of dual personality. As was stated earlier, his academic record was above average, and he did have a few close friends. DS Dunes has yet to interview the two ex-girlfriends. Even Henry's military record was described as above average. No disciplinary issues. After being discharged from the service, Henry went to London and attended night classes on botany at the local community college. What he did during the days has yet to be determined. While he was in London, his parents passed away and left him their cottage in Cockernhoe. After graduating from college, he moved back to Cockernhoe and seemed to be living the life of a retired army officer. After a time the Beavington's senior gardener abruptly left so they hired Mr. Chestermere. He had become accepted as part of the community.

Since DS Dunes spoke to a psychologist about dual personalities, he felt certain Mr. Chestermere was definitely hiding something. But what? DS Dunes decided it was time to bring Mr. Chestermere in for further questioning.

"Thank you for coming in so soon," stated DS Dunes as he enters the interrogation room. "I don't understand why you couldn't come out to the estate," grumbled Mr. Chestermere. "I just have a few more questions," stated DS Dunes. "Do you agree to this meeting being recorded" asked DS Dunes. "Yes, let's get on with it." grumbled Mr. Chestermere, "you know I have an estate to run."

"Firstly, where were you born and raised?" "Don't you already know that" snapped Mr. Chestermere. "Yes, but I want to hear it from you, to be sure the information I have is accurate."

"I was born in London, but when I was about four years old, we moved back to Cockernhoe. I later went back to London to attend Oxford University. After graduating, I entered the military and was sent to fight in the Suez Crisis. Once I left there, I came back to London to took some night courses in botany. During my time in London, my parents passed away and left me their cottage. I moved back to Cockernhoe and was later hired by the Beavington's because their gardener left abruptly. The rest you know." "How did you find life after leaving the services" asked DS Dunes. "Any problems?" "I coped, I had classes to help keep my mind off things. It was relaxing to learn how to care for plants and maybe even bring any that were failing back to life." Stated Mr. Chestermere. "Is it because of what happened during the Suez Crisis, that you decided to study botany" queried DS Dunes.

"The fact that your best friend died and you couldn't help him even though you did your best under the circumstances." "I tried, so hard," groaned Mr. Chestermere. "If only I had the resources, I could have saved him." "Why didn't you have the proper resources?" asked DS Dunes. "It seems that our upper-class soldiers needed their English tea and snacks, that there was not enough money for other things." "It was the rich people's fault that my friend and many others die. I hate them." DS Dunes noticed the hate and anger in Mr. Chestermere's eyes and voice. "Are we about done here?" asked Mr. Chestermere in a rather quiet voice. DS Dunes realized he had just witnessed the duality in Mr. Chestermere. It goes along with what the psychologist said. "What did you do about it, "asked DS Dunes, "Did you ask your senior officers about the lack of resources." "I asked, but they just laughed and shrugged it off like it wasn't important. I vowed I would get back at him," growled Mr. Chestermere, "but he died during the next skirmish, so I laughed." "I vowed to take rich people down a peg or two, for those who died needlessly." DS Dunes had seen and heard enough for today, so he let Mr. Chestermere leave, reminding him that he may have more questions at a future time.

CHAPTER 14

"So what did you think of that?" DS Dunes asked DC Rainey as he was putting away the recorder. "Well, Sir I've never met anyone with split personality before, but if it hadn't been referred to by the college psychologist, I probably would have shaken my head if I had witnessed what I did just now," admitted DC Rainey. "Do you think one personality could be a murderer and the other one doesn't know?" queried DC Rainey. "I've got our researchers putting together some information on that subject that we can study," mentioned DS Dunes. "It will help us understand things.

Meanwhile, we will concentrate on those interviews of the ex-girlfriends. Also, we'll be keeping an eye on our Mr. Chestermere." added DS Dunes. Over the next few days, DS Dunes and DC Rainey were kept busy with the interviews and reading the huge amount of research provided for them by the researchers. DS Dunes also assigned a profiler to look into Mr. Chestermere's childhood. "I have the profiler's report," stated DS Dunes. As DC Rainey arrived at her desk the next day DS Dunes told her that he was a meeting that afternoon, he would like you to read the report, and they would meet up later at the Boar's Head Pub on Market Street at 5 p.m. for dinner and to touch base," added DS Dunes. "Evening Sir, I got us a table in the far corner so we wouldn't be disturbed," stated DC Rainey as

DS Dunes comes in. "Great idea," mentioned DS Dunes, as he takes off his coat.

"After we put in our order we will review then stop to eat," continued DS Dunes. "I want to get through the whole report tonight, and then we can refresh tomorrow morning." "That dinner was just what I needed, now to work." "What are your thoughts?" DS Dunes asked DC Rainey as he takes out his writing tablet. "Well, I can certainly understand why a person develops a split personality, after what Dr. Ogden reported on Mr. Chestermere's childhood. Do you think his parents had any idea what he was going through? Maybe they could have sought professional help for him, and then the Beavingtons will still be alive." commented DC Rainey. "So from what the report says, it is not Mr. Chestermere's fault if he did kill them. Where do we go from here? DC Rainey asked DS Dunes with a puzzled look on her face. "I read that we can have a potential suspect to undergo hypnosis, then, we can ask specific questions. It would have to be approved by a Judge and agreed to by Mr. Chestermere and his solicitor because he intends to hire one once he feels we are seriously looking at him for the murders. I would also request he go through a psychiatric evaluation. We would have to tread carefully." admitted DS Dunes. "There would have to be at least two psychologists present." "If Mr. Chestermere thinks he is innocent, he probably won't ignore our request for the hypnosis, because he would have nothing to lose," added DS Dunes. "Do you think a person with split personalities has any idea of their affliction? I guess then they would go for therapy on their own.

But if he knew, then he may try pleading not guilty because of insanity." questioned DC Rainey. "It would be good to get this case closed," added DS Dunes as he reaches for his coat. "We will pick this up in the morning. Have a good rest of your evening, DC Rainey," mentioned DS Dunes. "Thanks, you too, Sir," added DC Rainey as she follows him out of the pub. Once outside DC Rainey hesitates and asked DS Dunes, "If Lord Chestermere is convicted, one way or the other, then it would be Gina and Arthur inheriting, wouldn't it, Sir?" asked DC Rainey. "I would think so." answered DS Dunes, "but we cannot go forward until after the judge has reviewed the psychologists and the psychiatric reports," continued DS Dunes. "In the meantime, we have some paperwork to finish then we will have an early night or two. The hypnosis will take place in 2 days as well as the psychiatric evaluation."

CHAPTER 15

In the conference room, DS Dunes and DC Rainey are reading the hypnosis reports and the psychiatric evaluation of Mr. Chestermere. "What is our next move, Sir?" queried DC Rainey. "It's obvious from these reports that we can charge Mr. Chestermere with the murders of the Beavingtons." Stated DS Dunes, "then a judge will set a court date, and a jury will be selected," he answered. "Now we get the warrant and bring Mr.Chestermere in. Then I will have to inform Sr. & Jr. Keyes that they will have to be in charge of the estate until the trial is over, however long that may take." An officer hands DS Dunes the warrant. "Let's be off, Detective Constable," said DS Dunes. An hour later, they are back with Mr. Chestermere in handcuffs. "I want my solicitor," he demanded. "It's my right." "We had trouble locating him." offered DS Dunes. "He'll be here as soon as he can.

Meanwhile, you can wait for him here," announced DS Dunes as he shows Mr. Chestermere into an interrogation room. "Would you like something to drink," he asked Mr. Chestermere. "No," yelled Mr. Chestermere. "I just want my solicitor." "He will be brought in as soon as he arrives," answered DS Dunes, as he leaves the interrogation room. He then sends a team to search Mr. Chestermere's property. "It looks like Mr. Chestermere's solicitor requested a private chat with his client," added DS Dunes, after he peeked through the interrogation room two-way mirror.

"We can go across the square for a cup of tea while we wait. What do you say to that Detective Constable?" asked DS Dunes. "I can really use one, thank you, Sir," added DC Rainey. As they leave DS Dunes informs the front desk officer that they would return in an hour.

Back in the interrogation room, DS Dunes prepared the recording equipment while Mr. Chestermere sits and glares at him. DS Dunes looked around and said, "Let us begin. Mr. Chestermere, you have been formally charged with the murders of the Beavingtons. Were you read your rights,?" he asked. "Yes, I have," growled Mr. Chestermere. "Has your solicitor explained what happens next and that you will remain in custody until your first appearance in front of the judge?" continued DS Dunes. "He did," answered Mr. Chestermere. DS Dunes looks towards Mr. Chestermeres solicitors and says, if there is nothing else, we will have an officer escort your client to a cell. "What next, Sir?" questioned DC Rainey. "Well, you can go home early and enjoy some family time, I have to finish this paperwork," stated DS Dunes, as he points to a stack of files on his desk. And this stack, we'll tackle tomorrow. Some cases seem to get pushed aside when there has been a murder. Thank goodness a majority of these are open and shut, the time-consuming part is the paperwork. Goodnight officer and thanks for your hard work." added DS Dunes.

The next morning when DS Dunes arrived, he received a note saying that the jury selection would begin this week. He also received the report of the search his team made of Mr. Chestermere's property. They found a few containers of what they think is plant food and sent them to the lab. He should receive their report in a few days.

He finds DC Rainey up to her elbows in paperwork. "Morning, Sir," she said, "I thought I would get a head start on this lot, as she points to a stack of files." "I saw Mr. Chestermere's solicitor at reception," mentioned DS Dunes. He's here to confer with him. Did you know that his trial starts in two weeks?" "The sooner it starts, the sooner it will be over," stated DC Rainey. "I was just going to get myself a cup of tea, would you like one, Sir?" "Thanks, we'll see if we can get to the bottom of these stacks by the end of our shift," added DS Dunes as he sits down and opens a file.

"Sir interrupts the desk clerk. There is a Sr. Keyes here to see you." "Put him in conference room #1," said DS Dunes. "I'll be right there, and please bring us some tea and biscuits."

"Hello Sr. Keyes announced DS Dunes as he walks into the conference room. Thank you for coming down at such short notice. I will only keep you a moment. How are things at the Estate?" "Fine," answered Sr. Keyes, "I tell you this took all of us by surprise. What can I do?"

"You will need to take over the running of the Estate while Mr. Chestermere is away. I know you planned to retire, do you think Jr. would be able to step into your shoes?" queried DS Dunes. "For something this complicated, I don't think so. How long do you think this will take?" asked Sr. Keyes. "That is hard to say," replied DS Dunes. "I have known murder trials to take weeks and even months, so we will have to wait and see. Whenever you need to speak with Mr. Chestermere about Estate affairs, you will have to contact his solicitor, stated DS Dunes as he handed the card to Sr. Keyes. Thank you again for coming," he stated, as he escorts Sr. Keyes to the exit.

As DS Dunes returns to his desk, he stops by DC Rainey's desk and asks, "How is the progress, Detective Constable." "Coming along, Sir," she answered. "I can actually see the bottom of this stack."

"I just received the results of the lab test on the containers found at Mr. Chestermere's." mentioned DS Dunes." the contents match perfectly with the plant food that killed the Beavingtons. It seems like Mr. Chestermere made the poisonous batch but kept it in a container that was for regular plant food. He would bring the poisonous stuff to the greenhouse, and the Beavingtons would use it, not knowing the dangers. After they died, Mr. Chestermere replaced the poisonous containers with regular ones. Then he did the same for Alicia. It meant that Mr. Chestermere put some thought into the murders.

It doesn't coincide with the fact he suffers from dual personality. He could be faking that. But the hypnosis pointed to the fact that he does suffer from a malady similar to that. I will need to speak to the psychologists again.

"We also found some papers carefully wrapped in plastic and stuffed in one of the empty plant food tin." Points out DC Rainey, as she hands the evidence bag to DS Dunes. He puts on evidence gloves and opens the bag. After a few minutes he exclaims, "now we know how Mr. Chestermere found out that he is Mary Beavington's half-brother. Here are his birth record and some letters from the Beavington's solicitor reminding Mr. Chestermere's mother what she agreed to. It seems Mary's father had a thing for one of the housemaids and got her pregnant. That maid was Henry's mother, and as per the times she was dismissed from her position. She lived with her aging parents in London for about four years; then moved to Cockernhoe; where she soon married a man several years her senior; Harold Chestermere. Harold adopted Henry, and a few years later, he died in a farming accident. He left everything to Henry and his mother."

CHAPTER 16

When the staff at the estate heard that Mr. Chestermere was under arrest, they were in shock. They also heard that there was a search of Mr. Chestermere's property. To imagine that he worked with them daily and they wondered if they might have been in danger at some point. It was frightening to think about what could have happened. Was it true, they asked themselves? Mr. & Mrs.Locke were trying to stay positive until they received some news. They also knew that Gina and Arthur were worried, by some of the comments they made at dinner last night. Mr. Locke had called Sr. Keyes and was told that he would be coming in a few days to explain the situation, but until then, that they should carry on as usual.

When Sr. Keyes arrived, all he saw were anxious looks. He knew what he had to tell them would not dismiss those looks but hoped it would relieve some of their anxiety about their futures.

"I know you are all concerned about your futures, but until the trial is over, you really must try to carry on as usual," stated Sr. Keyes, in as comforting a voice as he can. "What will happen to us if he goes to prison?" asked Mr. Locke, who was sure he was talking for them all. "Who will inherit? What will we do? Will we have to move?" he asked hesitantly. "I'm not at liberty to divulge that information just yet," replied Sr. Keyes. "We all have to wait for the trial to be over.

I know it's not much consolation. You will still receive your wages. Mr. Lock, I have some papers here authorizing you to be in charge of the household matters and along with Arthur's help, I am confident that both of you can keep up with the grounds. Charge anything within reason to this account." He added as he handed Mr. Locke some papers. "And if there is an emergency, contact my office. I'm sure you will be alright," he added. "I have complete confidence in you. I will keep you informed of the trial proceedings. They are now selecting a jury, and once that is completed, the trial will commence. I do hope my visit has relieved your minds somewhat." stated Sr. Keyes as he prepared to leave.

"Well, what do you think": Mrs. Locke asked her husband? "I feel a bit better, but we are no further ahead than before. We will be alright," she added as she looked around at the others. Gina looked like she was going to cry, but Arthur did look a bit more relaxed. Mr. Locke turned to Arthur and said, "We have to talk about the work we have to do on the grounds. Do you want to meet after lunch? Once we have a plan, I think we'll all feel better." "Sure," answered Arthur. "I will be in for lunch shortly." He announced as he left. The Lockes returned to the kitchen for a short meeting while preparing lunch. "All will be well," quoted Mr. Locke.

After lunch, Arthur and Mr. Locke went outside to take stock of what has to be done and any supplies necessary.

Inside, Mrs. Locke and Gina did the same, especially the larder. Mr. Locke cautioned that they would only buy what was essential. Once the lists were completed, Mr. & Mrs. Locke enjoyed a cup of tea, while Gina and Arthur each went their own way. Gina went to the greenhouse, where she sat to remember the Beavingtons. She also remembered some occasions when Alicia was rude to her. Gina whispered, "I forgive you" to the last plant Alicia was nurturing. She then sat and cried for a while.

Meanwhile, Arthur was walking around the grounds remembering things he helped Mr. Chestermere repair. He remembered that Mr. Chestermere wanted things done perfectly; he used to say, "that's how I would do it if it were my property." Arthur didn't pay much attention at the time, but knowing what he knows now, it made more sense. He did understand "wanting" it to be perfect if the land was his. Sr. Keyes had called with some news. The jury was selected, and the trial would begin the next day. He suggested that they all try to keep positive thoughts and carry on as usual. He would keep them informed as the trial continued.

CHAPTER 17

During the jury selection, Mr. Chestermere was very demanding of his solicitor, Mr. Evans. He insisted on certain foods to be delivered, which had to be pre-approved by the judge. He also expected to have a private cell, which was approved, due to some possibility of him harming his cellmate. And then he would complain about having to sit in on the jury selection. Everyone was happy when the trial date was set; even Mr. Evans. There were seven women and five men on the jury.

The first day of the trial will be Monday, August, at 9 a.m. DS Dunes had informed Sr. Keyes who in turn informed those on the estate.

Mr. Chestermere was very upset when he entered the courtroom. He was yelling at the guards that he had an estate to oversee, and why was he here. The guards were very relieved when they had settled him in the prisoner's box. The bailiff announced, "Please stand, the court is in session, My Lord Duncan presiding."

DS Dunes was in the courtroom on the first day. He was to be a witness for the police department. When Mr. Chestermere heard his name, he got so upset that the guards had to restrain him. During DS Dunes testimony Mr. Chestermere kept his head down and could be heard muttering to himself. Mr. Evans saw the looks the jurors gave

Mr. Chestermere. They probably thought he was off his rocker and had already made up their mind as to how they would decide.

After DS Dunes' testimony, the judge adjourned the court for the day. It will resume tomorrow. Mr. Evans had a short list of people who knew the young Mr. Chestermere, who were to give testimonies.

At the estate, Mr. & Mrs. Locke were discussing if it would be appropriate for them to attend the trial for a day or two. They would go to his sister's in London since Arthur would take over the running of the estate, and then he would be able to go to London once the Lockes got back. He would stay at his grandmother's.

But, later that day, Mr. & Mrs. Locke were presented with a subpoena to be witnesses for the defense, and that they would not be able to attend the trial until after they testified. It said that they needed to be in court in 2 days and meanwhile Mr. Evans suggested that they not talk to anyone else about the murders and Mr. Chestermere. It appeared that Arthur and Gina also received subpoenas. Mr. Locke assured Mrs. Locke that their testimony would be a character reference since they knew and worked with Mr. Chestermere. Mr. Locke called Sr. Keyes, who advised him to tell the truth and try not to worry.

On the third day of the trial, the Lockes and Arthur had were questioned. They then decided to stay one more day before returning to the estate.

There was someone overseeing things, but the sooner they got back to the estate, the sooner they can resume their routine. Sr. Keyes promised to keep them informed as to the outcome of the trial.

CHAPTER 18

A fter five days of hearing testimonies, Mr. Evans rested his case. He had decided not to put Mr.Chestermere on the stand; because of his erratic behavior. He was sure the jury had already decided as to what their verdict would be.

The prosecution's first witness was DS Dunes. Since his earlier testimony for the defense, his team had found some containers at Mr. Chestermeres that proved he planned the murders. DS Dunes explained to the court how Mr. Chestermere would mix up a poisonous batch of plant food and put it in an empty container that had a label saying it was regular plant food that the Beavington's always used. They had no reason to think it was different; both had similar odors. DS Dunes believed that since it was pre-meditated, it could not be a result of dual personality. The next witnesses for the prosecution were the psychologists who performed the hypnosis and the psychiatrist. Even the prosecution decided not to call Mr. Chestermere.

By the end of the day, the prosecution also rested their case. Judge Duncan adjourned court until next morning when both sides would present their closing statements. Next morning both sides presented their closing statements, the judge informed the jurors of their responsibility and adjourned court. The jurors were sequestered overnight. They resumed deliberations the next morning and by 3 p.m. they had come to their verdict.

Court had resumed, and Mr. Evans and Mr. Chestermere were asked to stand to receive the verdict. "Have you come to a verdict?" the judge asked the lead juror. "We have your Lordship." announced the lead juror. "What say you?" asked the judge. "We the jurors find the accused guilty of all three counts of murder." The lead juror replied. The judge thanked them, and then dismissed them. "Given the lateness of the day, we will adjourn until 9 a.m. tomorrow to receive the sentence." announced the judge. The very angry Mr. Chestermere was led away, yelling that everyone was against him, even his solicitor.

The next morning Mr. Chestermere walked into the courtroom looking defeated. He must realize that he won't be Lord Chestermere; nor would he ever be lord of the manor. The bailiff announced "all rise, the court is in session, my Lord Duncan presiding. Please be seated. Mr. Evans and your client, Mr. Chestermere, please remain standing." added the judge. "Mr. Chestermere, after reviewing the psychologists' reports and witness reports, and witnessing your behavior these past few days, I have concluded that you do have an issue. Therefore I sentence you to life in Bethlehem Royal Hospital. You will be required to attend counseling sessions as set up by your doctor who will be obligated to send reports regularly that you are attending and participating in said sessions and what your progress is.

Your solicitor was briefed of further information, and he will explain everything to you on his first visit at Bethlehem." stated Judge Duncan. "Bailiff, please have Mr. Chestermere removed from court and prepare him for transport to Bethlehem. The bailiff announced," the court is adjourned." Mr. Evans assures Mr. Chestermere he will be visiting him the next morning.

At the Bethlehem Royal Hospital, Mr. Chestermere was given a tour of the premises, then had a session with the resident psychiatrist and informed of his schedule for further sessions and other activities he could get involved in. It was suggested that it would be for his benefit that he involves himself in as many activities as he can. After two weeks, Sr. Keyes visited him to see how he was faring and to inquire if he needed anything.

Sr. Keyes informed him that his cottage and belongings are securely locked up and if he wants to sell to please inform his office. Mr. Chestermere thanked him and congratulated him on his retirement.

CHAPTER 19

S r. & Jr. Keyes went to the estate to inform everyone as to the verdict and the changes that will have to take place. Sr. Keyes told them that Mr. Chestermere was sentenced to life at Bethlehem Royal Hospital after being found guilty of all three murders. And since the Forfeiture Act came into effect in 1982, Mr. Chestermere was legally disqualified from inheriting the estate, therefore, he had drawn up documents stating that Gina and Arthur would be co-inheritors, but since they were both under 21 years old, Mr. & Mrs. Locke were appointed legal guardians and would manage the estate until Gina and Arthur turned 21. In early spring, both Arthur and Gina had applied to attend college in London, Arthur to study botany and Gina to study for the arts. She always dreamt of being a writer and illustrator. They would both continue with their plans, but would both take a course in estate management, as well as learning all they could from Mr. & Mrs. Locke. They would both live in the students' dormitories at the college and come home on weekends and holidays.

Mr. Locke thought it would be best to have Gina and Arthur walk around the estate to get the lay of the land. They would need to know everything. Arthur does know quite a bit already since he worked there, but now he would see it as part owner, and Gina needs to know all about what is involved in being a co-inheritor.

After their tour, Mrs. Locke had prepared a nice tea where they would voice their opinions and ideas for their home. Arthur thought a chicken coop with layers and eating hens. This way they could have enough for them and some for needy villagers. Gina mentioned that it would be a good idea to enlarge the present garden, with the same idea Arthur had. Mrs. Locke then took them on a tour of the house. After that tour, Mr. Locke thought it would be a good idea for them both to present any ideas in the form of a proposal, and then they would research their ideas both in a practical aspect and a financial one. Afterward, Gina and Arthur went off on their own, each with a note pad and a thoughtful look.

Arthur's idea for a chicken coop wouldn't cost too much. There was that abandoned shed by the garage. He would be able to set it up on his own. And Gina's idea to enlarge the garden would require hiring a lad or two from the village. Gina and her mom would do the planting. Both projects would be up and running before Arthur and Gina had to leave for London. All that was needed would be to hire a groundsman and someone to come in the mornings to tend to the garden.

Sr. Keyes arrived at the estate to check up on how things were and to give them an update on Mr. Chestermere. He said that Mr. Chestermere was finally settling into a routine. It seemed that he had accepted his fate.

Also, this would be Sr. Keyes last visit since he was officially retiring next week. Jr. has agreed to oversee the estate's interests. He had a good conversation with Gina while they were all walking around the estate showing Sr. & Jr. Arthur and Gina's plans. Both Sr. & Jr. found that the plans were an excellent idea and said that they were already thinking as estate owners. Jr. asked Gina if he could call on her once she gets settled in her studies. She looked at him with a shy look and said that she would look forward to it. Jr. left later with a big smile on his face.

9 781728 324432